LEGENDS
OF THE
SEMINOLES

LEGENDS
OF THE
SEMINOLES

as told by
Betty Mae Jumper
Illustrated by Guy LaBree

Foreword by James E. Billie
Introduction by Peter B. Gallagher

Pineapple Press
Sarasota, Florida

Inquiries should be addressed to:
Pineapple Press, Inc.
P.O. Box 3899
Sarasota, FL 34230
www.pineapplepress.com

LIBRARY OF CONGRESS
CATALOGING-IN-PUBLICATION DATA

Jumper, Betty Mae, 1923-
    Legends of the Seminoles / by Betty Mae Jumper with Peter
Gallagher. — 1st ed.
        p.   cm.
    ISBN 1-56164-033-6. — ISBN 1-56164-040-0 (pbk.)
    1. Seminole Indians—Legends. I. Gallagher, Peter, 1950-
II. Title
E99.S28J85   1994
398.2'089'973—dc20   93-50571
                                                CIP

First Edition
10 9 8 7 6 5 4 3

Design by Frank Cochrane Associates
Composition by Cynthia Keenan

Printed in Hong Kong

CONTENTS

Chief James E. Billie and his son Micco

$\mathcal{F}$OREWORD *by James E. Billie*

When the Creator, the Grandfather of all things, had finished creating the earth, there were many things he wanted to put there. Birds, animals, reptiles, insects, many different living things.

The Creator did have certain favorite animals. He particularly liked the Panther, Coo-wah-chobee — crawls on four legs, close to the ground. The Panther would sit beside the Creator and He would pet the Panther, over and over, across its long, soft, furry back.

The Creator made sure that certain animals and plants possessed unique healing powers. When the Creator touches certain things longer than normal, His powers automatically go into what He touches. He told the Panther, "When everything is complete, I would like for you to be first to walk on the earth. You are majestic and beautiful. You have patience and strength. There is something special about you. You are the perfect one to walk the earth first."

Creator went to work making all sorts of animals and birds. Animals on all fours, animals with hooves, animals with paws, birds with claws, insects, reptiles — why, there was nothing the Creator left out.

When the earth was ready, Creator put all the animals in a large shell. Or something round. He set it along the backbone of the earth — the real high mountains. "When the timing is right," He told the animals, "the shell will open and you will all crawl out. Someone or something will crack the shell and you must all take your respective places on the face of the earth." The Creator then sealed up the shell and left, hoping the Panther would be first to come out.

Time went along, and nothing happened. Alongside the shell stood a great tree. As time passed, the tree grew so large that its roots started encircling the shell. Eventually a root cracked the shell. The Panther was patient, which the Creator liked. But, at this particular time, Panther was too patient. The Wind started circling around the crack in the shell, round and round the inside, so vigorously that the crack was made larger.

The Wind, however, remembered that the Creator wished for the Panther to be on earth first. "We will fulfill the Creator's wishes," said the Wind, reaching down to help the Panther take its place on earth.

The Wind was everywhere. The Wind was the air we breathe. After Wind helped the Panther out first, the Panther thanked Wind for the honor.

Next to crawl out was the Bird. The Bird had picked and picked around the hole, and, when the time was right, stepped outside the shell. Bird took flight immediately.

After that, other animals emerged in different sequences. Bear, Deer, Snake, Frog, Otter. There were thousands of others, so many that no one besides the Creator could even begin to count them all. All went out to seek their proper places on the earth.

Meanwhile, as the Bird was flying around looking for a place to live on earth, the Creator was watching. He watched each animal and did not intervene, but left the animals on their own. The Creator often allows things to happen along their own sequences. Sometimes a thing must happen on its own merits.

When the Creator saw that all was done, He decided to name the animals and put them in clans.

For being such a good companion, the Creator rewarded the Panther with special qualities: "Your clan will have the knowledge for making laws and for making the medicine which heals," Creator told Panther. "You, the Panther, will be in possession of all knowledge of different herbs. The Panther will have the power to heal different ailments and to enhance mental powers."

Creator believed the actions of the Wind were very honorable and noble, so He told the Wind: "You will serve all living things so they may breathe. Without the wind — or air — all will die.

"From this day forth, Wind will be brother to the Panther and all living things. When the Panther is making official medicine, the Wind must be there, beside the Panther, no more than a few paces away from the Panther at all times."

The Bird, for being able to take flight, will be ruler of the earth, said the Creator: "The Bird will make sure that all things are put in their proper places on earth."

So this is how the beginning was made. Some call it the Creation. Though there were many, many animals put on this earth by the Creator, all came to know their proper places on earth.

Today, among the Seminoles and other Indian people, there are ceremonies on the occasion of the greening of the earth. At these ceremonies, you can see the Panther, with brother Wind, mixing the medicines for all people to use.

If you enter the festival grounds and don't know your place, you seek out the head of the Bird clan — usually a man ranked high within the clan — and you ask where to make your camp. He will ask you "What is your clan?" If you say "Panther," he will give you a direction and instruct you to seek out the head of the Panther clan and he will tell you exactly where to sleep.

Stories such as the Creation and many other legends do have important meanings to us. Sometimes, however, interpreting the legend may confuse us. Seminoles, Miccosukees, Creeks, Cherokees, Choctaws, and many other tribes tell tales of Creation. These stories may parallel but are rarely told in exactly the same manner from tribe to tribe. For good reason — they all live in different locations on the earth and that has much to do with the way the stories are told.

Dr. Betty Mae Jumper comes from the Muscogee of Creek origins and also speaks the Miccosukee language. As a child, she learned the Muscogee versions and her legends, while parallel, may differ slightly from the Miccosukee versions.

The recipient of a legend must do his or her best to retell the story as close to the original version as possible. It is a great responsibility and for this reason, the best storytellers are greatly respected among those in the tribe.

We retell the same great stories over and over and over and over, just as we have been doing since the Creation. Today, however, we have the privilege of writing, recording, and videotaping. This may eliminate the continuous human retelling, but, at the same time, there is no misinterpretation. Each word is exactly preserved. In this way, we can enjoy the original version told by the storyteller.

I've had the special privilege to hear, with my own ears, these legends and stories from Betty Mae Jumper's own mouth. I hope I will be lucky enough to hear more, even the same legends, over and over again. I never get tired of them.

James E. Billie, Chairman
Seminole Tribe of Florida
Chokoloskee
March 1994

Betty Mae Jumper with her grandson Jorge Chebon Gooden

INTRODUCTION *by Peter B. Gallagher*

ABOUT THE LEGENDS

The office of the Storyteller can be found inside an old, low-slung duplex just beyond the right-field fence of the Seminole Indian ballfield. Betty Mae Jumper's office window, lined with steel bars, looks out over a tall chain-link fence near the southern edge of the tribe's urban Hollywood reservation.

From this vantage point, the Storyteller can watch a yawning world crawling through time. Amid distant sounds of traffic and children, lazy brown mongrels lie next to mobile home trailers, mockingbirds flutter about the water oaks, and obstinate crows squawk at tomcats sulking in the shade of the unkempt hedgerows.

The dogs outside Betty Mae's window walk on all four legs. The crows are black. And neither mockingbird nor reservation cat have been known to speak in human voice. This may seem logical, but the world of the Seminole, as portrayed through Betty Mae Jumper's stories, can easily spin into a strange and unpredictable dimension.

Take the Little People, for example. You can't really see Little People, but they live in the holes of the oldest gnarled oak trees, Betty Mae says. Look close. Kind of squint your eyes and try to see them running all around the twisted wood. Don't be scared of them, but don't hassle them either. It's not that Little People are specifically evil or anything, but they have certain ways of doing things. If you go with the Little People, your time is short.

And, if none of this is making any sense, then it is time to consult the Rabbit. But watch out! Rabbit is a liar, Betty says, Rabbit's a liar, but Rabbit knows.

The first time I came upon Rabbit and his lies, the rascal was all crumpled up and slid under a leg of Betty Mae's desk. No one has ever seen the actual surface of this desk, but it is presumed to be wood and is located in the tiny Editor-in-Chief's office just to the right of the Tribal Communications reception area.

In the center of this hallowed anteroom,

11

across from boxes of palmetto husk dolls and hand-carved balsa tomahawks, buried somewhere beneath a mound of varied and exotic clutter, is the place where the Storyteller works.

Only a working journalist, facing perpetual deadline, could truly appreciate the Storyteller's desk. It is part museum, part landfill, part gift shop, part library, a veritable mound of archaeology that exists in that nether world between the Smithsonian and the Smith Family Robinson. What Betty Mae Jumper needs to know is in the vicinity of this desk; whether she can find it or not is another story.

Here there are news releases, tribal government reports, phone messages, pamphlets, and research notes. There are cattle reports, powwow flyers, and photos — some taken this week, others taken in the late 1920s when Betty Mae and her family first migrated to this part of Florida. There are dolls made by Minnie Doctor, patchwork pot holders, little bows and arrows, and boxes full of tiny canoes.

Letters, invites, requisitions, resolutions, her framed honorary doctorate of humane letters from FSU. Books, paperwork, clippings, handwritten logs. Notes scrawled in margins hidden in forgotten files. Receipts, bills, folders, and musings — bits and pieces of a colorful life spent documenting, interpreting, collecting, and preserving. This great mass of memorabilia rises and falls in foothills of flotsam, spilling onto the floor in plops of junk and history.

The day I found out about Rabbit, I was standing in this office, across from this great desk, watching Betty Mae Jumper at work. Her head was barely visible behind a stack of reports as she toiled busily away, signing this, shuffling that, alternately dropping things on the floor, answering the phone, and shrieking for "Twila!" "Virginia!" and other members of her *Seminole Tribune* staff.

Sitting quietly nearby, absolutely stoic in her colorful patchwork dress, was one of the many female tribal elders who hang out with Betty Mae Jumper everywhere she goes. Occasionally, Betty would look up and say something in the difficult Miccosukee language. The woman would nod, but never speak.

Absentmindedly toeing through a pile of paperwork near the desk, I spied something old and handwritten poking out from beneath. I tugged at the crumpled, water-stained sheet, but it was stuck under the leg. The familiar scrawly handwriting of Betty Mae Jumper was all over the page. I peered closer: something about a rabbit. And a lion.

"Excuse me, Betty," I said, as I lifted the desk and kicked the Rabbit's tale out. Several mounds of important stuff slid off onto the floor, and she glanced up in irritation. I picked up the brown-stained sheet of paper, blew off the dust, and held it up for her to see. "But what's this?"

"Oh my goodness, that's a Seminole legend. I've been looking for that," Betty Mae said, grabbing the Legend of the Rabbit and the Lion from my hand. Suddenly my eyes became adjusted to the light of what Betty Mae Jumper was doing. I began to see similar sheets of hand-penned prose, like sparkles of gold in a mine shaft, all over her desk and office floor — the mortar holding her mound together. I pulled up another one and held it toward her eyes. It was titled, simply, "Seminole Do's and Don'ts."

"I forgot about that."

As the muse had hit over the years, Betty Mae Jumper had been translating from Creek and Miccosukee and writing down, in longhand English, the legends and stories of her childhood. And filing them about her desk. She didn't really know why she was doing it, just that it needed to be done.

"These stories are very old, but have never been written down," is how Betty Mae rationalized her deed. "If the oldest people on the reservation were to die, without leaving them for others to learn, then our culture would be gone, too."

Like most Seminoles from her generation, Betty Mae Jumper is intimately familiar with the old Seminole legends and stories of childhood. Many of her fondest memories recall the quiet and simple family times, accented by the gripping fables which have meant so much to her life.

"It was always at night, when it was cool. There would be a campfire and we kids would be under the mosquito nets," she recalls. "They would tell us stories, to teach us and to help us go to sleep. My uncles, my aunts, my mother, and grandmother all told stories. It was mostly the older people who told these legends to the children."

Most of the stories Betty Mae remembers had to do with "a time when the world was very young. A time when the animals talked and walked on two feet," she says. "This was in the very beginning, before Jesus was born."

So deeply ingrained were the characters and plots of these folktales that Seminole children related to them much like children today relate to television cartoons. Fantastic as they were, with talking animals and profound natural events, these stories provided a comfortable consistency in the lives of children forced to contend with the clashing cultures of dual worlds.

The Seminole Indians of Florida were one of the very last American Indian tribes to begin interacting with the outside world. By the 1920s, they were scattered about the rural wilderness areas of south Florida in small camps and villages on both private and reservation lands. Some lived in houses and had jobs. Most lived in traditional cypress and palm thatch chickees and survived in abject poverty, subsisting on lands that no longer produced the game or crops that had maintained their forebears.

Government assistance was sporadic and disorganized. From a policy of removal and roundup prior to the Civil War, the United States had embarked on a mission to assimilate this country's indigenous peoples into the white man's mainstream. With great fervor, church missionaries followed this bulldozer, infiltrating Indian tribes all over North America, pushing aside tradition and culture to let in the Word of God.

The Florida Indians are direct descendants of the last remnants of the legendary Seminole Nation — a combination of Creek and other tribes chased from indigenous southeastern homelands into Florida during the early 19th century. The name "Seminole" was formed from the Spanish word "cimarron" (wild) combined with the Muscogee term "se-mi-no-li" (runaway) to give unified substance and identification to the multicultural, multilinguistic, multiracial groups Andrew Jackson made it his destiny to destroy.

When the dust had settled from three undeclared Seminole wars — the most expensive military campaign in the U.S. — most of the Seminole Indians had been deported to Oklahoma or left dead along the infamous mid-1800s "Trail of Tears." The rest — historians estimate 100-300 men, women, and children — had disappeared into the impenetrable swamps and strands of frontier Florida. The U.S. military finally gave up and left the last ragtag groups isolated in the river of grass. They remained there, unconquered but unwanted, mistrustful of the white man and his government for nearly half a century.

At first, the Florida Seminoles emerged from hiding only to trade pelts for supplies at remote outposts — like Ted Smallwood's trading post in Chokoloskee — where they were granted trust and acceptance. Later, when the wilderness shrank and roads appeared, Seminoles were seen on the roadsides, selling palmetto trinkets and wrestling alligators for the tourists. By the 1920s, hand-operated sewing machines were common in Seminole chickees and a small signature industry offering the colorful patchwork Seminole jackets and skirts was born.

It wasn't until the mid-1950s, when facing the federal policy of termination, that a movement born from within nudged the Seminoles from their disenfranchised funk. Old wisdoms combined with new ideas and a constitution was batted out during miracle debates beneath a giant oak tree in Hollywood. In the summer of 1957, the official Seminole Tribe of Florida received federal recognition.

Five years later, a splinter group of Florida Seminoles won their fight for separate recognition as the Miccosukee Tribe of Indians of Florida. Their brothers, sisters, aunts, and uncles who where forced to the Indian territories out west remain today as the Seminole Nation of Oklahoma. Separate entities, never to be rejoined.

The eerie session in the cool of the night. The dancing shadows of flames on the storyteller's face. The living wonders of the dangerous world. Each bizarre episode in the legends is bracketed by an inherent common sense. Of course the sun hates people; they are always screwing their faces up when they look skyward. Well sure, bears used to be men. They still walk upright, even today. God is the Breathmaker. Think about it. Any child who's heard a screech owl knows something about that sound ain't good.

These tales became a vital means of passing on tradition, teaching moral lessons, facilitating child development, molding character, and . . . well, they were just plain entertainment in the absolutely mundane world of the swamp Indian. More than anything, the myths sought to create bonds with the surrounding environment.

The Seminole legends echo the universal patterns of mythology found in cultures all over the globe. The Big Lake is Okeechobee, where the dragon snake lives. But the great monster also lives in Loch Ness. And the Cherokees have a water serpent living in a Lake of Spirits high in the Smokey Mountains.

No matter which culture examines it, if corn is harvested, an ugly woman scraping the kernel scabs from her legs is somehow

involved. And the Rabbit is the trickster, the liar, the public-address announcer, the half-supernatural wonder worker in European folklore, Korean animal myths, and in the mythology of just about every tribe east of the Mississippi.

Very little educated criticism has been directed to the legends of the Seminoles. While the Eastern Cherokees developed their own alphabet in the 19th century, the Seminoles stayed hidden from the 1840s until well into the 20th century, almost totally isolated from the outside world. During this time, the Seminoles developed a unique subtropical Native American subculture that remained unblemished, a good deal longer than that of most tribes, by the white man's arrogant conquest of the frontier.

Where the Oklahoma-bound Seminoles, Cherokees, Choctaws, and other eastern tribes were forced to leave behind the familiar scenes and localized surroundings that framed their mythology, the Florida Seminoles stayed home — in the Village of Many Indians, on the edge of the Big Forest, watching the Bashful Star.

THE STORYTELLER

Betty Mae Tiger was born April 27, 1923. She was delivered into this world by her grandmother, Mary Tiger, and a white woman named Sis, beneath a palmetto thatch roof in a birth chickee east of the Big Lake, about a quarter mile into the Big Forest from the Seminole camp at Indiantown. Her mother was Ada Tiger, a full-blooded Seminole and a member of the Snake Clan; Ada had been sent away from the village to have her baby, as was the custom in those days.

"It was believed that when a woman has a baby, she was to go at least a quarter of a mile away from the camp. At this spot, other ladies would prepare a shade for her or build a small chickee for her so she could deliver the baby there," wrote Betty Mae, in an essay which has never been published. "Men and boys could not be around at this time, only the Medicine Man was allowed. The ladies would put a pole in the ground and bend it toward the woman so she could hold onto it during labor.

"After the baby was delivered, the mother and baby were bathed and put to bed. This bed had been made by the other ladies. They would stay in this place for four days and four nights. One lady would stay and cook for the new baby's mother. On the fourth morning, the mother would bathe again. All of the clothing she had used during this time was thrown away.

"The mother could not be around men and boys for four months. She would eat alone during this period. On the fourth month, the baby's hair would be cut off, and it would get new clothes and a new name."

The father of Ada Tiger's baby girl was a white man, a French trapper and cane cutter who lived nearby and traded with the Seminoles. In 1923, in that part of the world, among these particular people, a half-breed was cause for alarm. The fear and hatred of the white man still ran hot in the blood of tribal leaders and medicine men. Sons of the runaways, their entire lives had been a bitter dance on the crumbling edge of a doomed world.

"All half-breeds were killed. If a girl got mixed up with a white man, she was beaten up and whipped. Some could not get up for days after the beating. They would kill the white man if they caught him around the Indian girl," wrote Betty Mae. "In the early 1920s, half-breeds were still being killed. They would put mud in the baby's mouth to choke it. Or just throw the baby in the water. The government finally stepped in and stopped it."

The Indiantown Seminoles were a particularly rough and traditional bunch. They were direct descendents from the war band of irascible Billy Bowlegs, who single-handedly started the Third Seminole War and was the last Seminole war leader to be deported to Oklahoma. This was a man who perfected the art of ambush and run. Openly cooperating with the white man's system was not one of Billy Bowlegs' character attributes.

Further complicating the changing world of the Seminole was the specter of Christianity in the swamps. The 1920s saw the first circuit-riding preachers infiltrate the heathen Florida Indians. It was a dramatic, divisive time. Some medicine men were easily convinced; others would not throw down their medicine bundles.

The Tiger family of Indiantown were early converts and great friends with the famous Oklahoma preacher Willie King. His spiritual guidance proved a source of strength throughout Betty Mae Jumper's life. With great difficulty, she learned to maintain an unspoken, enigmatic balance between the seemingly opposite concepts of The Word and her Seminole culture.

In this atmosphere, it was no surprise to her great uncle Jimmy Gopher that the Indiantown villagers would want to kill little Betty Mae. Late one night, primal fire in their eyes and the swirl of the medicine man in their conscience, a throng demanded the half-breed's death. A man to be reckoned with, however, Uncle Jimmy had been ready since the day she was born. He and Grandpa Tom Tiger answered their shouts with a smoking shotgun.

Though the bullets worked to save the child's life on one night, the persecution would not go away. Ada Tiger packed up her family and moved south to join other Seminoles in the "big city" village at Dania, in Broward County. Eventually, the entire Indiantown camp would disband. Faced with impossible circumstances, Betty Mae's father had left for the West long before; she sought to stay in touch, however, and, from a distance, the white side of her family has followed her career with pride.

Much of the turmoil which surrounded her formative years was lost on young Betty Mae, who was barely five years old when her family left Indiantown.

Betty Mae Tiger was 14 years old on her first day of school. She began her education as a fourth grader at the Cherokee Indian Boarding School in North Carolina. At the age of 22, she became the first Seminole

Indian to graduate from high school. In those days, Florida public schools did not admit Seminole students.

"Oh, I wanted so much to go to school. But they told me I could not because I was an Indian," Betty Mae remembers. The irony was not lost on a hall full of dignitaries at Florida State University recently when Betty Mae gave a keynote address — just after she was awarded an honorary Doctorate in Humane Letters.

Death, the sadness of a newborn baby dying in the wilderness, is what fueled Betty Mae Jumper's fire for education. As a very small child, she accompanied her mother — a midwife — on her rounds. "Sometimes, she couldn't save the babies. I thought, there must be a way to save them," said Betty Mae.

She came to a sober realization that helped her cross over the line of traditional belief: "We had a lot of good medicine men, but they could only go so far."

After graduating from a nursing school in Lawton, Oklahoma, Betty Mae returned to south Florida to work at Jackson Memorial Hospital in Miami. Counting her lengthy service to various Seminole health programs, Betty Mae spent over 21 years working in the health profession. The series of buildings which house the Hollywood Reservation medical clinic is named the Betty Mae Jumper Complex.

Petite, dark-haired, with deep, beautiful eyes and a quick smile, the young Betty Mae had the looks and demeanor of a movie actress. "When I was a young boy, I used to think she looked like Susan Hayward," says James Billie, a protégé who would become chief of the Seminoles in 1979. "She was a very attractive and shapely woman. Every man on that reservation wanted to be with her."

It was dashing war hero and Seminole alligator wrestler Moses Jumper, Jr., however, who won her heart. They were married in the winter of 1946, a storybook couple. A brilliant and charming man when he was sober, Moses Jumper fought a lifetime battle with alcoholism. Though he often became unruly and uncooperative,

Betty Mae stuck by her husband through 46 years of marriage.

When her husband couldn't rise in the morning to wrestle alligators at nearby tourist attractions, Betty was known to take his place, fearlessly sitting on the back of the scaly leviathans and spreading their jaws for the tourists. Strong and selfless, she herded cattle, raised three children, took care of many sick tribal members and spent nearly every available free hour in the pursuit of various tribal affairs and projects.

"My mother is one of the strongest people I know," says Moses Jumper, Jr., her oldest son, the tribal recreation director and a published poet. "She has suffered a lot in her personal life. But she never gives up. I'd have to say a lot has to do with her strong faith."

Her greatest skill was that of an interpreter, a trusted translator of the new ways to the old people. At a very young age, she became fluent in three languages: Creek, Miccosukee (the two distinct Seminole languages), and English. She acted as a critical bridge over the language barrier during the raging times when the tribe sought to gain both federal recognition and peace within itself.

In 1966, she was chosen by her peers as Seminole Tribal Chairman, one of the first elected female Indian chiefs in the country. By his own definition, James Billie was a "go-fer boy running all over learning politics from the grassroots" at the time of Betty Mae Jumper's election to the top Seminole office: "I found out the Seminole Tribe had $35 on the books, zero balance in the bank. We were in trouble. This woman stood up. She took hold of that old buffalo. By the time she left the chairmanship, there must have been over half a million dollars in there!"

She founded three tribal newspapers, the *Seminole News* in 1958, the *Alligator Times* in the mid-1960s, and the *Seminole Tribune* in 1979, the year Chairman Billie assigned her the job of Director of Tribal Communications.

As Editor-in-Chief of the *Seminole Tri-*

bune, Betty remains a controversial figure among her peers. Her acerbic writings — criticisms of Seminole government, complaints about non-Indians taking Seminole jobs, tirades against alcoholism — are balanced by her sentimental memories of Seminole old days and the occasional preachy Christian lecture. Those who raise the ire of Editor-in-Chief Betty Mae Jumper may find their picture left out of the *Seminole Tribune* — as several politicians have learned.

On weekends, at powwows, folk festivals, and Indian events all over Florida, Betty Mae Jumper's booth of Seminole arts and crafts is a familiar sight. Dozens of tribal elders make their only income handmaking items for Betty Mae's booth. She holds court on a folding chair behind her colorful display of dolls, beads, jewelry, clothing, and toys.

Since the 1960s, at the urging of the legendary Southern tale-teller Cousin Thelma Boltin, Betty Mae Jumper has been performing at storytelling workshops hosted by the state of Florida. She is featured each May at the prestigious Florida Folk Festival in White Springs. Her high, monotone — often sing-song — recitations mimic exactly the rhythms and timbres vocalized by her great aunts and grandmother around the cool night campfires.

In 1991, Chairman Billie asked that Betty be videotaped telling a few of her stories to Seminole children at the tribe's Big Cypress Ah-fach-kee Indian School. From this session, the semi-animated video "The Corn Lady" was produced.

Perhaps it stemmed from her tenure as a newspaper editor, but Betty Mae went even further than telling Seminole stories in public. She began writing down as many as she could remember. Since this collection was put together, I've begun to notice more sheets of paper strewn about her office.

"It's my life story," she explains. "And some more legends I remembered."

Betty Mae Jumper herself is a subject of Seminole legend and lore. One of the best was recounted recently by a Seminole man who remembers when Betty was the unofficial tribal truant officer, scouring the reservation each morning for kids skipping school.

"Betty Mae Jumper was known to always get her man," said Christopher Osceola, who remembers hiding in the cow pasture one morning.

"One minute I could see her driving a van down the road. The next minute she was driving right through the pasture, that van bumping up and down, her head banging off the roof, the cows running one way and us running the other. We ran like hell.

"But everywhere we turned, she was there. We finally gave up and she hauled us back to school. Gave us a shower and brought us into school. I still don't know how she did that."

THE ARTIST

When I asked Betty Mae Jumper about an artist to illustrate her legends, she had two ideas. The first involved a long trip down several dirt roads, through the woods south of Immokalee, to the camp of the Independents.

The Independent Seminoles exist in an obfuscated time warp, a few dozen stalwarts defending aboriginal rights that long ago fell out of the lawbooks. Grim, stoic, and very traditional in spirit, they are true 20th-century enigmas. The Independents live the old ways as much as possible, but most drive modern pickup trucks and operate answering machines in their chickees. They revere the power of Indian medicine but, when they are really sick, go to the non-Indian doctors and hospital like anyone else.

They have refused membership in either of the organized Seminole or Miccosukee tribes. Though most subsist at poverty level, they steadfastly refuse to collect more than $1 million now held for them in trust by the federal government — their unwanted take from the controversial land claim settlement awarded the Seminoles in the late 1980s.

It was high noon when we pulled into the small camp of chickees and pickup trucks. Betty's honking horn had apparently wakened the artist. Groggy and squinting in the sunlight, Paul Billie walked out of his chickee. Behind him, I could see his artworks — sketches on plain paper — strewn all over the dirty wood floor.

As he approached us, barefoot and barechested beneath a bright Seminole jacket, I felt excited. For here was certainly an artist who could draw the great serpent the way the Seminole imagined it. Or the Little People.

Shaking hands, I explained the purpose of our visit. He seemed alarmed as I spoke and physically backed away from me when I held up the typed manuscript for this book. He refused to touch, or even look at, any of the written legends. A ghost somewhere had overtaken his eyes and I didn't understand.

Betty Mae stepped forward and talked with Paul for a long time in their native language. He seemed to calm down and brought out several of his latest drawings, two of which Betty Mae purchased on the spot. I found out later that Betty was his benefactor; she holds the largest single collection of his original artwork. When we turned to leave, Paul gave us a lusty wave goodbye. Neither of us would see him again; Paul Billie died of pneumonia a few months after our visit.

As we left, Betty Mae told me that Paul could not illustrate her legends. It was his belief that the legends told by the elders should never be written words, especially in the white man's tongue. "He said it was bad medicine," said Betty Mae. "He was afraid to touch the papers you were holding."

Betty Mae Jumper was undaunted; she had been walking this tightrope since her birth. She quickly mentioned her other idea: "Why don't you call Guy LaBree?"

When Guy LaBree entered the first grade at Dania Elementary School in 1946, he quickly made friends with some unusual children: the first generation of Seminole Indians to attend Florida public schools. These rowdy, dark-haired children didn't like wearing shoes and neither did LaBree; from this simple bond was forged a deep relationship between the man known today as "The Barefoot Artist" and the unique culture he has dedicated his career to preserve.

The Seminoles' nearby Dania camp was located about 22 miles north of Miami. It had once been known as Big City Island. In the 1800s, this area was a remote oasis of isolated high ground surrounded by the wet Everglades — a perfect hideout for Seminoles running from the U.S. military. By the end of World War II, the Everglades were being drained and the Big City Seminoles found themselves forgotten, aliens from another era, hemmed into a world of change and transition between the creeping urban jungles of Ft. Lauderdale and Hollywood.

LaBree would often sneak away to the Seminole camps, eat frybread, and sip sofkee with the grandmothers of his friends. The Seminole kids would hike to the LaBree family home and marvel at the running water. They would translate the stories told by the old people, scatological references and all; he would let them drink iced tea by the pitcher and stand in his shower as long as they wanted. He would spend weekends at their Seminole camp, lying at night and watching the stars; they would spend weekends at his house, playing the hi-fi, acting like urban teenagers, and staying up all night.

LaBree's easygoing nature was not threatening to the Indians; he was treated like family on the reservation and given access to ritual and ceremony few white men had experienced. Though no one realized it at the time, the Seminoles were rapidly losing their culture; it was disappearing beneath the language, religion, and urban sprawl of the white man.

"I never took a note. I never made a

sketch. I looked at a lot of things and never realized what I was looking at," says LaBree, whose years as a Seminole "insider" faded away when he reached high school. "We all grew up together. But then, they went to one high school and I went to another. And I got interested in girls."

Though he dabbled in oil painting in high school, LaBree went into the printing business after graduation. He married, raised three children, and found himself depressed and wearing shoes, working 80 hours a week. He only rarely saw his Seminole pals anymore. The seed that would bring LaBree back to the Seminole reservation was only germinating.

In the late 1970s, Guy LaBree couldn't take it anymore. His work life was hunching over a light table in a dingy backroom print shop. Such work came easy to Guy and the money was big, but boredom was taking a toll. Something inside Guy LaBree was bursting to get out and he was having trouble keeping it caged. Wife Pat reached into her husband's past and suggested a familiar therapy: "Why don't you take up painting?"

It did not come back easily. Guy removed his work shoes, retrieved the same gooey palette he used in high school, and began painting flowers and mountain scenes, clouds, and fruit. "I was painting everything I had seen everybody else do and the paintings came out awful." The colors were there and the hand-eye coordination soon returned, he says. But the soul was missing.

One day an old friend, Seminole tribal member Alan Jumper, stopped by. The Seminole listened to his friend's frustration. To Alan Jumper, the solution was simple: Paint the ways of the Seminole; preserve on canvas the vanishing culture that Guy LaBree had witnessed in his youth.

Something clicked in Guy LaBree's brain while his Seminole pal talked: "I thought to myself, I should be able to do that. Look what I already knew. But then I found out I didn't really know anything."

Undaunted by criticism from Seminoles, obsessed with research and accuracy, tireless in the pursuit of both fact and fancy, LaBree took advantage of a prolific urge to paint the Seminoles. Freeing himself from the constraints of the print shop, he imagined himself in his own paintings: surrounded by the smoke and fire and screams of a great battle, dizzy with fear in the whirlpool sucking dugout canoes. He became the panther waiting on the deer, the warrior waiting for the ambush. LaBree's careful brush brought it all — and himself — back to life.

Well, not all. "My rule is, if there is something secret, I don't put it in there," he says. "I have been halfway in the middle of painting something and a Seminole will say, 'I don't think you should do it. That's not well known,' and I've stopped right there. I respect that. I don't take it any further. So you see I've got 20 or 30 paintings in my mind I can never do."

From his tiny studio in the Arcadia hinterlands, Guy LaBree produced all the paintings for this collection. LaBree's return to the world of art has now stretched over more than two decades, and his intensely researched, richly colored portraits of Seminole history and culture are national treasures. These works are part of Seminole culture now; they have more than stood up to the challenge of preservation his Seminole pal gave him years ago.

LEGENDS

OF THE

SEMINOLES

TWO HUNTERS

"I remember my mother telling this story. It was her way of teaching us 'Don't ever eat anything out of place.' In other words, if you find candy, don't eat it off the ground. A lot of these stories are to teach children something important to learn."

On the edge of the Everglades lived two men from the Village of Many Indians. These two men were hunters who went into the Glades for months at a time. Sometimes, when the hunting was good, they came back to the village within two weeks or less with lots of meat which they would smoke and dry. They hunted deer and birds and picked up as many water turtles as they could fit into their two canoes. They only hunted when they had to, when the meat supply had run out.

23

Early one spring, the two hunters talked about the Big Lake and how there would surely be lots of game around there at this time of year. "We will return in two weeks or less," they assured their families. "Now is a good time to hunt near the Big Lake."

They left in the morning and, on the second day, made camp near the Big Lake. On the way, the two hunters talked about how the hunting would be good, for they saw many animals around eating the green grass. After making camp, they settled down to sleep.

As the sun rose the next morning, they hurried out and immediately killed a deer. It took most of the day to clean the large deer. They dried and smoked the meat so it would keep until they returned home. Both men were filled with happiness and good feelings for they were sure there was plenty of game around and this trip away from the village would be short. They would return soon with lots of meat for their families.

They went to sleep early. When they awoke the next morning, they were surprised to see that it was raining very hard. The rain fell most of the day, so they stayed at the camp. In the late afternoon, the rain finally stopped and the sun came out. "It's too late now to hunt," said one hunter. "I guess we'll have to wait until tomorrow. I think I'll take a little walk along the lake."

The other hunter was feeling hungry, so he cooked some deer meat. Soon the hunter returned carrying two big fish. "Look what I found," he said. "Beautiful bass, big and fat."

"Where did you get those fish?" asked the other hunter. "I didn't see you take anything to fish with when you left."

"No," the hunter explained. "I found them jumping on the ground near the lake, so I picked them up. I guess they must have come down with the rain!"

"Go and put them into the lake," said the other hunter, "and let us eat the meat I am cooking."

"Oh no," his friend replied. "These fish are too good to throw away. I'm going to clean and cook them right away." And he did.

After the meal, they sat around the fire and talked. They agreed to start early the next day and maybe kill two deer and fix them before nightfall. Soon it was time to go to sleep. All the night birds were singing away. Somewhere near, in a tree, an old owl was laughing and crying throughout the night.

In the middle of the night, the hunter who ate the fish called and called, "Come here! Come here!" His partner awakened and yelled out: "What's wrong?" He stood up and walked over to his friend's mosquito net. He stared in fright as his friend spoke: "I think I'm turning into a snake. You told me not to eat that fish but I didn't listen to you. Now look at me!"

The hunter started a fire to get a better look at his troubled friend. His legs had already turned into a snake's tail!

"I want you to go home. Don't wait to see how I look. You can't help me now," said the man turning into the snake. "By daylight I will be completely turned into

24

the shape of a snake. Go home and tell my wife and children what has happened to me. Also tell my parents, sisters and brothers. Tell them when the moon is full to come and see me.

"Bring all my family to the lake. Remember the big log near the lake? I want you to hit it four times when the sun is right in the middle of the day. I want them to see me and I want to talk to them. Tell them not to be afraid. I won't hurt them. Now go! Get out of here and run home!"

The other hunter left without looking back, taking with him the meat they had prepared. On the second day he reached the Village of Many Indians and told his friend's family the bad news.

Then the day came for the hunter to take his friend's family to the lake. They arrived at the lake beneath the full moon and camped out, waiting nervously for the next day. Finally, when the sun reached the middle of the day, he led them to the big log and fulfilled his friend's request. He hit the log once, twice, three times, four times.

When he was finished, bubbles came up from the middle of the lake. Then up came the head of a large snake. The children were scared, but the older people told them to be quiet and listen to what the snake had to say. The snake floated to the top of the lake and slithered near the shore where his family stood.

Slowly, the snake moved toward them. "Come close," said the snake. "It's me. I wish to talk with you. Listen close to what I have to say, for after this I will never speak again."

When they had all moved close, the snake began to speak again: "I did wrong when I cleaned those fish, cooked them and ate them. I knew better, but I went against the forbidden law of our elders. I am paying for it now. When you leave, I want my family to never think bad about me. Think forward and go on with your life, for I will never be back. This lake is going to be my home. I will live in this water until I die. When you all go, never come back to this lake, for once you all leave, all my memories will be gone. I won't know you at all. I might be mean and I might hurt you. It is the life of a snake I'll be living. Just remember all the good things and forgive me."

The snake turned to his hunter friend: "I want you to please help my family and share meat with them. Teach my sons to be good hunters like you. Make sure they take care of their mother." The hunter friend promised he would.

"Now," said the snake, "I'm coming to the top. I want you to see all of me." And when he did, everyone could see that he was huge, longer than a large canoe. Then, suddenly, the snake went underwater. When he came back up, he was back where he started from, in the middle of the lake. The snake stuck his tail high out of the water and waved it at them. Then he went down deep, deep into the black waters of the Big Lake.

With sad feelings, his family turned and left the Big Lake, never to return again.

ALLIGATOR

"The Seminoles would never harm or kill an animal, except for food. When my great uncle told me he was hunting for deer or turkey or gopher, why that was exactly what he came back with. And no part of the animal was ever wasted. Now, alligators were a little different because we had sport with them. We used to drag them out and have a game to see who could put one to sleep first. The Seminoles have always played with gators even though they are dangerous."

When the world was new, there was only one language and all living things understood each other. So, when there was a gathering, everyone would come — birds, people, animals, just any living thing. They would all come to perform their talents to show off and see who was better than who.

Among them was a rabbit who was not much of a performer. He was walking along the lake, looking for something to do, when he came upon an alligator with his mouth open, facing the sun. The rabbit hopped on over, kicked the alligator, and asked, "What are you doing?"

"Ha!" said the gator, "don't you know I'm drying my mouth to kill germs?"

The rabbit thought about this, then sat

27

down to talk awhile. He asked the gator if he could hear the songs and dancing at the gathering. "Oh yes," said the gator. "I hear."

Then the rabbit suggested they move closer to the dance area. "All right," said the gator, who followed the rabbit toward the grounds.

When they got closer, the rabbit suddenly picked up a stick and started beating on the alligator until he ran back to the lake.

A few days later, the rabbit again went for a walk and ran into a squirrel wearing a pretty jacket. The rabbit asked if he would loan his jacket, but the squirrel said, "No. I don't want to loan it to you!" But the rabbit has a way to get the things he wants, so, somehow he got the jacket from the squirrel.

"Don't forget to come back with my jacket," said the squirrel, as the lying rabbit ran away. It wasn't long before the rabbit came upon the alligator in the same place as before.

With the jacket on, rabbit looked a lot like squirrel. The squirrel/rabbit went right up to the gator and said "Hello!"

"Hello," said the gator, "and goodbye. Away with you. I was beaten by your kind the other day."

"Really? Who was it?" asked the squirrel/rabbit.

"The rabbit," snarled the alligator.

Squirrel/rabbit then asked alligator how he could be killed.

Now, the gator didn't know the rabbit had borrowed the squirrel's jacket. "Well," said the gator, "first you hit my back and I can't move. Then if you hit me on the head, it will truly kill me."

"Oh!" said the squirrel/rabbit.

Then the squirrel/rabbit said, "Gator, do you see that hill? Why don't you get on top of that hill. You could be closer to the sun and it would make you dry faster."

The gator thought that was a good idea, so he began to climb the hill, still not knowing that it was a lying rabbit dressed in a squirrel's jacket.

"I'll come with you and talk with you," said the squirrel/rabbit.

"OK," said the gator. Away they started up the hill. But before they got to the top, rabbit picked up a stick and hit the alligator on the back. Then, rabbit hit alligator on the top of the head and the gator fell and died.

So, if anyone wishes to kill an alligator, this is how it is done.

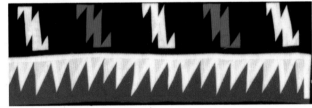

BOX TURTLES

"We call them yuk-che-po-luk-skit, little round turtles. We'd find them all the time crawling on the road, or in the dry areas. They were real good to eat. Two or three of them would make a whole meal. We'd roast them, turning the turtle upside down on the fire until it was cooked."

Once, when the land was new, all creatures spoke in one language and understood each other. In the village, when a cow was killed, anyone who wished to get a piece of meat could do so, for the meat was shared by all.

On the hillside lived a family of box turtles. The old mother turtle heard about the beef, so she told the father to go and get a small piece of meat so they could all get a taste of it.

Away went the father turtle to the place where the cow was being cleaned. All there greeted the father turtle and he sat beside those who were waiting for the meat. Finally, when the meat was cleaned and cut up, everyone began choosing the parts they wanted. When it came the turtle's time, he was asked what he wished to take.

"Do you want a piece of leg?" he was asked.

"No," answered the turtle. "If I ate the leg, my legs would ache."

"How about the ribs?"

"No, my ribs would ache."

"Liver?"

"No, my liver would hurt."

On and on and on, each part they offered brought the same answer from the turtle: he would hurt if he ate that part. So, they said, "Away with you," and they all left with all the meat that had been divided.

After everyone was gone, the father turtle opened his eyes and saw that they had left the blood clot lying around. So he gathered all the blood clot and took it home. When mother turtle opened the package and saw what was in it, she got so mad that she threw it all into father turtle's eyes.

And that is why all turtles have blood-shot eyes today.

C OON

"The raccoon meant business to the Seminoles. They would sell and trade the hides for food and other supplies. I had a little raccoon pet when I was a girl and it would follow me everywhere."

One late afternoon, an Indian hunter was sitting by the fire cooking his dinner meal. As he finished eating, the Indian hunter heard noises coming from a far distance. The voice seemed to be saying, "Round and round lay my barrel, round and round lay my barrel. When I get there I will drink it."

The hunter was thirsty and he thought to himself, "A barrel of drink would be great. Why not?"

The voice was moving nearby, passing behind a cypress tree and into the sawgrass. The hunter arose and began to follow the voice. He stayed behind so he wouldn't be seen. The voice was moving fast, but the hunter was able to keep in step with the sound.

The voice moved such a great distance that the hunter began to grow tired. Fi-nally, however, the voice quieted down and the hunter moved closer. He peered through the brush and saw a little raccoon washing his paws and face in the cool waters of a little brook. The coon bowed down to take a deep drink, stood on his hind legs and looked around. Then he sang again:

"Round and round, black stripe on my tail, I will lay on it after I drink and get home."

What the coon meant was that when he got home from hunting and eating shrimp, he would take a drink from the brook of cool water and climb high up the cypress tree where he would lie on his tail with the black stripe that went round and round.

In the words used by the coon, the "barrel" sounded like the black stripe went round and round his tail. To the man, hearing at a distance, it sounded like he was saying, "a barrel of drink will be laying there and when I get home, I'll drink it."

Oh, the hunter was so mad, because he came a long way following the voice of the little coon, thinking he was going to get a drink from him. Slowly, disgusted, the Indian hunter went back to his camp.

THE CORN LADY

"This is the legend of how the corn came to the Tribe. I can remember my grandmother telling us this one at night by the campfire. Sometimes we were under the mosquito net ready for sleep. Other times we were eating sweet potatoes and roasted oranges. On a cold weather night, those hot oranges were real good."

There once was a family living at the edge of the Big Forest, a wonderful place with swamps full of meat and fish. The family had places to grow vegetables, pumpkins, potatoes, beans and tomatoes. They also raised pigs and cows. These were happy people with no worries — they had everything!

The children could be seen running about everywhere, playing around and swimming in the ponds nearby. But sometimes, when the older children were playing really hard, they would forget to keep an eye on the younger children.

One day an older sister put her baby brother down to play with the little children while she played with the older ones. They played a long, long time and she forgot about her baby brother. When she finally went to check on him, he could not be found anywhere. She called and called and called his name but could not find him anywhere.

The big sister ran home to tell her mother. Soon, all of the women in the village were out looking for him. They kept looking until sundown but were unable to find the baby. When the men of the village returned from their Big Forest hunting trip, they all looked for the child well into the night. But no baby was found.

A few days later, the men returned to hunting and fishing. The father of the baby sent for the wise medicine man. Since he lived quite a distance from the village, it took the medicine man two days to get to

35

the village at the edge of the Big Forest. When he finally arrived, he asked everyone to sit down. He told them about the "unseen people" that lived on small islands deep in the swamps.

The medicine man believed that one of these "unseen people" had picked up the baby and run off with him. He told the village people that they could not find these "unseen people." But, the wise medicine man believed that the baby was still alive someplace in the Glades. The family was very sad at this news and gave up looking for the baby and all hopes of ever seeing him again.

Years went by. The missing boy's family still lived in the same village. The brothers and sisters had grown up and some were married. Then one day a strange thing happened out in the jungle in the heart of the Everglades on a little island. No one had ever been there before, nor had anyone ever seen the place.

On the island was a beautiful camp with three chickees: one for the campfire, one for sleeping and one for eating. An old witch lived there and she had a young boy living with her. Every day she would prepare corn sofkee and vegetables for the boy. He soon grew to be a strong teenager.

The old witch was so ugly that it made you wonder where she came from. But her love for the boy was great and she raised him well. She knew that someday she would have to tell him the truth about himself. This made her very sad because she knew this day was very near.

The boy noticed that the chickees were old and falling apart and often asked why he was not allowed to repair them. The witch would never give him a reason. The boy questioned where she got the corn she prepared for him but she would never tell him. All he knew was that there was always plenty of corn to eat.

The day came when the boy decided it was time for him to follow the old witch. She would always get up very early, check to make sure the boy was asleep, pick up her basket and walk toward the swamps. One day the boy pretended to be asleep until she had gone, and then he followed her. She walked quite a distance to a cool running stream where she stepped in and scrubbed her legs until they were very clean. A little further away, she sat on a log, dried her legs and started rubbing them from the knees to the ankles until beautiful yellow corn fell and filled her basket. She continued doing this until her basket was full.

On the way back, she stopped and filled up another basket with white sand. The boy was watching her all this time. He ran back in front of her and quickly jumped in his bed and pretended to be asleep when she returned. She built a fire and parched the corn in the sand in an iron pot. She then placed the corn in a log which was about two feet from the ground. The log was about seven feet long and 12 inches around. She pounded it up and down until it was ground into cornmeal.

When breakfast was ready, the old witch called the boy to come to eat. But he refused. The old witch went to where he lay and said, "You know, don't you?" The boy didn't answer and she asked again. Finally he told her that he had followed her that morning and saw everything.

"I knew this day would come," the old woman told the boy. She began to cry. "Yes, my son, you have given me much happiness all these years, but it is now time you returned to your people."

She then told him the story of how she had taken him years ago when he was just a baby. She gave him the name of his family and told him where they lived. She also told him it would take at least two and a half days to reach his home. She then gave him the necklace he was wearing at the time she stole him away.

"I am an old woman and my time is drawing near," she told him. "You must do as I say: Leave and don't turn or look back.

Just keep going! Tonight when the sun goes down, you must go to bed and sleep. When you wake up past midnight, you must get up and get ready to go.

"Go east toward the sun, and go past two big forests on the other side of the Big Lake. This is where your people live and you will find them there. Now, sleep, my boy, you have a lot of walking to do. When you get up, pick up the fire and throw it all over the chickees and run.

"Follow the trail we have walked many times and go. Run! Run! Run! Don't cry! We have had many wonderful years together and I have enjoyed seeing you grow into a fine boy. Get yourself a pretty girl and marry among your own people."

Somehow, the boy knew she meant well for him. She had been good to him and taught him everything he knew, including how to hunt. Past midnight, the boy got up, sadness in his heart. But he did as the old woman had requested. He threw the fire on the chickees and started running. He ran until he was very tired and started walking. He walked all through the night.

At daybreak, he passed the first big forest and continued walking until that evening, nearing the second big forest. He was very tired and wanted to rest because he knew he was near his village. He wanted to be rested before he saw his people.

The boy found a large oak tree and climbed up about midway to a large branch that looked like a saddle. He could sleep here without falling out of the tree. He awoke at sunrise with the birds singing all around. Feeling hungry, he climbed down from the tree to look for berries to eat. After eating the berries, he found fresh water to drink.

He continued walking until he reached the Big Lake the old woman told him about. The men from the village were on their way hunting and he quickly jumped out of sight as he didn't want to meet them yet. He knew the village was very near.

The boy continued walking until he saw many chickees. He climbed up in a large tree and watched the people until almost sundown. He wondered what he would say to the people about where he had lived for the past years. After a while he climbed down from the tree and started walking to the edge of the village.

The children saw him and started yelling, "New man. New man. Visitor." The older men of the village came out to shake his hand and talk to him. When he told the old men about himself, the old men remembered the story of the little boy who was lost long, long ago.

The boy then gave an old man the necklace he was wearing when he disappeared. "Yes, yes!" cried the old man. "I know your family." They slowly walked to the other side of the village, where a man and woman sat talking.

The old man placed the necklace in the old woman's hand. She stared at the beadwork for a long time and then looked up to say she knew the work. The old man then told her that this was her son, returned from being lost a long time ago.

The story was told over and over to everyone that joined the happy family around the campfire. They sat and listened all night long to the boy's stories. After many months, the village men decided to go and see where the boy was raised.

They left early one morning and were gone for about a week. When they returned, they told of finding the place where the boy was raised. Only now it was a patch of beautiful green corn that stretched all over the island. Soon, everyone went to see the corn, which was so yellow and pretty. The men gathered all the corn they could carry and took it back to the village with them. They saved the seeds and planted them year after year.

After the boy returned home and the corn was discovered, a Green Corn Dance was held every year to thank the Great Spirit for his blessing. And this is where the Indians got their first corn.

CROWS

"La-chee. The crows always want something they shouldn't want. My grandfather used to call them 'stealers of the corn.' Grandmother would put up blankets and old clothes that would flap in the wind to scare the crows away from the corn."

Once, among all the flying birds in the beautiful forest, were two special birds. They had very colorful feathers that shone brightly under the sun as they flew around. All the other birds admired and envied them. And the songs they sang were out of this world. When these birds sang, the others in the forest would quiet down and just listen to them.

One day, as these two birds were flying around, they saw a strange thing coming up in the air which was not a cloud. They looked and looked from up in the air, but they couldn't make out what it was. One said to the other, "Let us fly a little ways further and see what it is."

"I'm scared," said the other, but he followed his friend halfway to the strange thing. Then both stopped in a tree and looked and looked.

"What is that orange color below and that strange black color going in the air?" said the one bird, begging his friend to go closer. So, they flew right to the edge of where the forest was burning — something the birds had never seen before. They sat a long time watching it. Then one bird said, "Let us fly to that black tree and see the burning from the top."

The other said, "No. Let us go back. We have seen enough." But the other kept it up, wanting to fly to the top of the tall black tree. As usual, he won the argument and they flew to the top of the tree and tried to sit on a limb.

But the limb broke and the birds fell to the ground into the black soot which burned their beautiful feathers into charcoal.

And their voices were gone. They couldn't get any sound out, until one day they learned to say "Caw. Caw." For this, they were ashamed and never returned to the beautiful forest they once knew.

*T*HE DEER GIRL

"The deer has the most beautiful eyes. When I was chairman of the Seminole Tribe, my husband found a little fawn while he was hunting and brought it to me. It was Bambi and she lived with us for many years. I would never go hunting for deer. I was always too partial to animals. Even a little bird I wouldn't kill. When the hunters would bring the deer home, I wouldn't look at it. I ate deer meat when I was a little girl, but I would never eat it now."

A Big Dance and gathering was being held near Big Forest. These dances were held for four days and four nights. Everyone got all dressed up and made their camp near the dancing area.

The first night the Big Dance began with all the people dancing. There came a

41

beautiful girl with the most beautiful eyes. Every Indian there was watching her dance. She was perfect with her steps as she danced with her turtle shells. Before the end of the last dance, she disappeared into the darkness just before daybreak.

On the second night she appeared again in her beautiful clothing. One of the braves began to dance with her. He got in front and she followed. For two nights they danced till almost daybreak. But then she disappeared during the last dance. No one knew which clan or camp she was from.

People began questioning each other about her. Even the brave who danced with her had questions. She only told him that she had come to the Big Dance to enjoy dancing and wanted to keep on dancing. And to only disappear after the last dance of the night.

On the last night of the gathering the brave knew he had to talk to her. This was his last chance to express himself to her. He wanted to tell her how much he liked her and that he wished to marry her.

So he went to the girl and told her how

beautiful he thought she was, how her eyes would shine when she talked. He had never seen any girl with such beautiful eyes. But her answer was "I can't marry you. I am different from you."

"From what chickee do you come?"

She answered, "I don't live in a chickee." And she would give him no other real answers to his questions.

As the night was ending he began to worry more and more about the girl with the beautiful eyes. As dawn drew near, she began to move away from him. Again, she went into the darkness, only this time he followed her. She disappeared too fast, and by the time the sun came, the young man was alone in the forest.

Then he saw a fawn, a young deer standing there looking at him. And on the fawn he saw those beautiful eyes he had seen on the girl.

He knew then why she said she could never marry him. Swiftly this young doe disappeared into the thickness of the Big Forest.

When you look at the eyes of a deer, they are beautiful.

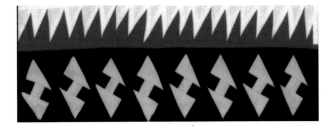

*T*HE EAGLE (I)

"We used to see the bald eagle every once in a while. It's a big, beautiful bird, but the Seminoles are kind of superstitious about it. To us, the eagle is a rare bird with a lot of power that could cause you trouble. The Seminoles don't wear the eagle feathers like the Indians out West. Every tribe has a different belief about this. To us, the panther was the strong medicine."

One day a man went out hunting and killed a deer. As he was skinning his kill he heard noises up in the sky. There he saw a big bird flying around. Quickly he dragged the deer under a log to hide it. But the eagle was so large, it came down, moved the log and carried off both the deer and hunter to her nest.

The little birds in the eagle's nest began eating the deer but had nothing to do with the hunter. Every time the mother eagle brought back kill, the hunter would tear off part of the meat for himself and dry it out to eat. He found water where rain fell in.

All the while mother eagle was perched up on the mountain above, watching her chicks growing bigger and bigger. Soon it

45

was time for mother to teach her young chicks to fly.

At that point the hunter realized that one day the birds would all leave the nest. He wondered what would happen to him.

There were days when the mother came back less and less to the nest. This was because her chicks were now grown and ready to leave the nest. The hunter took out a rope he had hidden. When the time came for the chicks to leave, he tied the rope around one bird by the neck. When the bird took off to fly, the hunter jumped on its back and away they flew. He also had a stick to hit the bird with so he could go down.

When they reached an area the hunter recognized, he hit the bird hard on its head so it would land. After the hunter jumped off, he told the bird to go, but he had to push on the bird until it got up and flew away.

The hunter then walked until he came upon the camp where he lived. Everyone was surprised to see the hunter again. They had thought he had been killed when he never returned from his hunting trip. He took them back to the tall tree to show them where he had been all this time.

*T*HE EAGLE (II)

"Eagle is a big bird with beautiful colors on his feathers. When he flies he spreads his wings and glides along with the wind. He glides along as if he owns the world. The eagle lays her eggs high up in the trees and feeds the young only what she kills, never wasting kill. This bird earned its respect from the Indians. Eagle feathers are displayed with pride by Indian dancers from other tribes.

Tales about eagles have been told in many ways by different tribes. This particular story was told to me by an elder of the Seminole Tribe when I was a girl."

Once there were children out playing in an open field near where the eagles lived. The children saw a big bird flying around them, so they all ran for cover — everyone except one little boy. The big bird came down and picked him up. As the bird flew higher and higher, the little boy began to cry. No one on the ground knew what to do. Then two teenage boys said they knew where the eagle's nest was.

In the meantime the boy had been dropped in the nest. The young eagles in the nest looked at the little boy and began pecking at him. He stopped crying and began to pat them on their heads. The little birds liked him and soon quit picking at him.

Mother eagle noticed that the little boy had lived through two days. The chicks did not care to eat him, so mother went hunting again for something they would eat.

While mother was away the two teenagers climbed until they reached the top of the hill. As they were getting ready to climb onto the tree, mother eagle returned. Afraid that they might get killed, the teenagers stopped and waited on a big rock, where they slept till the next day.

When the boys awoke on the next day, they noticed the mother eagle was getting ready to go hunting again. After she flew off, the boys hurried to the tree where the nest was. In the nest they found the little boy sitting with the chicks. They quickly picked up the little boy and slid down the rope they had tied up. Off they went to return the little boy back to his family.

Remember! The eagle is a strong bird that can pick up anything, even if it is heavy. Never underestimate what an eagle can do!

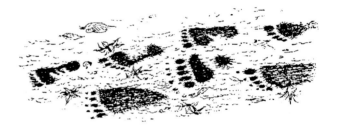 GRAY BEAR

"This was told to me by my grandmother, Mary Tiger. The bear was the biggest animal in the woods and there were a lot of them around in those days. Every once in a while, my uncles would go hunting for bear and we'd have a nice warm rug to sleep on. Remember never to put salt on bear meat — Seminoles say he'll come get you if you do."

Once there lived an Indian man who loved to hunt and bring food for his new bride.

Most of the time he would go with the hunters and hunt. But he would only stay away for a short time. One day the man thought it would be good to take his new bride along so he could hunt for a few weeks. She could dry or barbecue the meat as he brought it in.

The hunting was good. After they had been there a week, they had so much meat that the man said to his wife, "If this keeps up we can go home in another week or so." They both smiled to think that they didn't have to stay in the forest too much longer.

Another week passed, and the wife began to act funny. When the man returned from each hunt, he noticed his wife would be all dressed up, like when they married. At times, she would act mad and didn't want to be around him. She was not as happy as before.

He thought there must be something going on so he pretended to be heading for the Big Forest. But he hid and turned back to watch her from a distance.

She looked to make sure he was gone, then put on her new clothes and fixed herself up. She headed for the other side of Big Forest and he followed. She then stopped by a big tree and stood. A big gray husky bear appeared. The big bear walked slowly toward her.

Big bear stood up beside her and pushed her. She flipped over, and suddenly there landed a beautiful lady bear, the same color as the big bear. The two gray bears started running and playing until they disappeared.

The hunter returned to the camp and started packing all the meat he had and put it all into the canoe. She returned later that afternoon thinking that she would beat him back. But surprise! He was there!

The wife said she had gone for a walk. He then told her that he hadn't gone hunting but instead was watching her. "You can go on and do whatever you wish to do because I am leaving in a few minutes. I'm already packed. You could go back to the village and have the medicine man doctor you. But that's up to you."

He continued to pack up his things as she looked upon him. Without saying a word, she ran toward the Big Forest. As the man was going home, he passed through an open field. There, he saw the two bears roaming around. He knew then she had chosen to stay with the bear.

THE HUNTER AND THE BEAUTIFUL GIRL

"You should never camp around a graveyard. Where people are buried, you stay away, so that the people who are buried will stay there. After four months, the older kin will go back to the burial site to see and after that they never go back. That was the belief the Seminoles once had."

In most villages, the men were the ones who went out to hunt to supply their families with meat.

One day a man from one village told his family he thought it was time to go and find meat: "I'll be back soon if I kill a deer on the first day, but if not I'll return either in three days or four."

They lived near a river, so he rode out in a canoe.

He went many miles so he could find deer. This was an area where no one else had gone to hunt. It was almost sundown, so he docked his canoe, made camp, then went to sleep.

Early the next morning he set out again. He came upon some deer grazing and, of course, he aimed at the largest one and killed it.

The deer was too large to carry so he skinned and cleaned it right there. As he cut up the meat he hung some up to dry; this made even less weight to carry. What he didn't dry he barbecued right then. What he couldn't finish, he left for the animals to eat. He had noticed raccoons waiting for leftovers.

It was sunset by the time he reached camp. There he hung the meat high in a tree so the animals couldn't reach it while he slept. He built a large fire, cooked, ate and went to sleep.

As the hunter was dozing off to sleep, he felt as if someone walked toward the fire, then sat down. He peeked out from under the blanket and saw a beautiful girl sitting there. She was all dressed up with beads around her neck as if she was going to a dance or a wedding. He wondered where she might have come from. Was there a camp nearby?

She began to speak: "Hungry, hungry," she repeated.

The man had a long sharp stick he carried with him all the time. With this stick he speared some meat and gave it to the girl. He watched as she ate and noticed how hungry she had been. After a while, she got up and left without saying a word. She later returned, waking him by repeating the same old thing. It was almost sunrise. In the meanwhile the man kept the fire going, as he had become afraid of her.

Finally the sun rose and she left. He

said to himself, "I'm going to follow her and find out where she's coming from!"

In about 500 feet or so he came upon a bush that had meat hanging on it. This was all the meat he had given her earlier. As he looked around he noticed more. On some logs were beads, bones, pots and pans that must belong to her.

And there she was.

"Oh you," he said to her. "I thought you had eaten all the meat I had given you.

Instead you've wasted all of my food."

He then turned around and burned the bush that held all the meat. He returned to his camp, then headed back for home.

So whenever anyone goes out hunting in the Everglades they make sure, before making camp, that no one or nothing is around. For there are many graves scattered in the Everglades. The Indians never bury their dead all together. Instead they lay their loved ones wherever they see fit.

*L*ITTLE FROG

"When I think of my childhood, I remember that the nighttime was filled with the constant noise of frogs. The Seminoles believed the little tree frogs could tell you when it was going to rain. Now, I live in the city, on the Hollywood reservation, and I don't hear them at all. This story was told to me by my grandmother when I was just a baby. Where we lived, the sounds in the woods were very important to us. We were always asking, 'What is that sound from?' A lot of times we were answered with a story such as this one."

The little green frog was sitting on the edge of the water lilies, sleeping away. A big ol' rabbit came hopping along, came upon the frog and said, "Hi there! Why are you sleeping? It's too pretty a day to sleep. Wake up! Wake up!"

"I don't have to do anything," said the irritated little frog. But that big ol' pesky rabbit kept it up until the little frog got really mad and told him, "I'll fix you up."

So little frog started singing his funny little song or the noise he makes to call the rain. Within a few minutes, the black cloud came and the wind started blowing. Then the rains came and soaked the ol' rabbit so much he got cold and ran home.

Whenever you hear the frogs singing away today, better be near shelter, because they are warning you that rain is coming soon.

*L*ITTLE PEOPLE

"The older people used to tell us the Little People were in the Everglades and on the trees outside of camp. Later on, the seven dwarfs reminded me of the Little People, except there were a thousand Little People and they would all gang up and beat you. They used to scare us: 'Don't go out there by yourself or you might see the Little People!'"

When you get very sick the Little People appear at your bedside. No one but the sick person can see them.

They live in the holes of big trees. Thunder always chases and tries to kill them, but they run and disappear into the holes. This is the reason why you'll see lightning striking trees. The lightning will go around and around trying to get the little people. That is why there are so many holes in the trees.

The older people will always tell you never to stand under or against trees when there is lightning or you might get hit.

HOW LITTLE DOG CAME TO BE

"I love dogs. I was raised with chickens, cranes and dogs. I had one dog I'll never forget. Her name was Jeep. She was just a plain old dog, black and white, but my mother had trained her. If I strayed too far from camp, Jeep would grab my dress and drag me back home. I've had dogs ever since. They are a comfort to me. I talk to them. And they never answer me back."

Once upon a time there lived a family out in the Everglades. They had two kids and a little black-and-white dog who always barked at everything people were doing.

In those days there was only one language spoken, so everyone spoke and understood each other, even the little dog, who walked and carried himself just like a man.

Many times the father would go off and not return until late at night. So the mother told the little dog to follow the father and let her know where he went and what he did. "I want to know what all this walking business is all about," she said.

One late afternoon, father said, "Oh, well, I think I'll go for a walk" and away he went toward a trail that led around a big forest. The little puppy followed him but stayed a ways back so as not to be seen. They walked and walked until they came upon another village. There the father went and sat down and started talking with a girl who lived there with her family.

The little dog saw all this and hurried home to tell the wife what he had seen.

The wife was waiting up when the father returned. "So," said the wife, "did you have a nice long walk? What kind of skirt did you meet up with? Was it a deer-skin skirt or a bearskin skirt?" But she got no reply from him. Father knew she couldn't have followed him as he kept looking back to make sure no one was behind him.

Then he looked at the little puppy and realized it had to have been him. So he picked up the little dog and placed him on a log. There he sat and talked with the dog. "I know it was you! So you know what I'm going to do? After today you will never talk again, you will only smile and wag your tail. And you will walk on four legs as I am folding your paws."

The father was also a great medicine man. So he was able to do these things. And that is the reason why all dogs walk on four feet and can only wag their tails when they meet you.

63

THE LITTLE TURTLE AND THE WOLF

"When I heard this one, I pictured the wolf as a dog with its ears up. But I thought it was colored dishwater yellow. And you know I never heard a word about Little Red Riding Hood and the Big Bad Wolf until I learned about it in school.

Once upon a time a little box turtle was eating the fresh leaves of the green grass which had just popped out that morning. A wolf was out walking and came upon the little turtle. Wolf asked: "What are you doing, turtle?"

"What do you think I'm doing? I'm eating," said the little turtle.

After talking for a while, the wolf came up with an idea. He asked the little turtle, "Do you want to race?"

"What?" said the little turtle. "You know I can't run fast."

After standing for a while the wolf tried again: "Tell you what, little turtle. I'll let you start ahead first. Then I will come running after you."

But the little turtle said, "What's wrong with you, wolf? You know I don't run fast."

But the wolf kept it up until the turtle said okay.

The wolf pointed to a hill in the distance. "See that hill over there. I'll let you start off there before I come after you."

A date was set and the wolf left.

Little turtle said to himself, "Well, I'll teach that wolf. He thinks he's going to make me look like a fool and be laughed at. I'll show him."

Little turtle went and checked on where they would race. There were four hills until the end. "So I need four friends," said little turtle, who went off to find four of his

65

friends to help him out.

On the date of the contest, after sunrise, the wolf appeared underneath the big tree where the little turtle was sitting. "Are you ready?" asked the big wolf, laughing. "When I catch up with you I am going to stand on you. Ha ha."

Without a word the little turtle left to go stand on the first hill to start off. The wolf yelled at him, "I'll sleep awhile till you get on top of the hill and say you are ready."

Finally, the little turtle made it to the top of the hill and yelled, "I am ready!"

"Ha ha," laughed the wolf. "Let's have fun!"

Down the hill the little turtle went and the wolf came running. When he reached the top, the little turtle was going over the second hill. When the wolf got to the second, the little turtle was going over the third hill. When the wolf reached the third, the little turtle was already on the fourth hill.

At last the wolf reached the fourth hill and couldn't find the little turtle. The wolf looked and looked but there was no little turtle so he returned to the big tree and lay down. The little turtle was on top of the hill again, singing.

"Well, well, your bones will be quivering and the flies will be buzzing and buzzing around you."

At this, the wolf jumped up and chased the little turtle again. Same as before, the little turtle kept a hill ahead of him. Second hill, third hill, fourth hill, and then the turtle disappeared. So after the wolf was finished, he returned to his resting place under the tree again.

Wolf heard the little turtle again, standing on top of the hill, singing, "Wolf, wolf, your bones will be quivering and the flies will be buzzing and buzzing around you."

Once again the wolf became mad and ran, chasing the little turtle. But when the wolf reached each hill, the little turtle was always ahead of him, disappearing again after the last hill. Once again the wolf returned to lie down under the tree, very hot and tired and mad from all the running.

But there stood the little turtle singing again, "Wolf, wolf, your bones will be quivering and the flies will be buzzing and buzzing around you."

The wolf was so mad to think that this little turtle was still up on the hill singing about him. The wolf was tired, but he jumped up and yelled: "I'll get you this time, and when I do, you will be under my foot."

The wolf ran and got to the first hill. The turtle was on the second. When the wolf got to the second, the little turtle was on the third. And the same the fourth. The little turtle stayed a hill ahead of the wolf and then disappeared.

Wolf looked and looked down the hills and up the hills. Still no little turtle. The wolf returned to the big tree, hot, tired and exhausted. He dropped to the ground under the tree and just lay there. Again, the little turtle began to sing from the hilltop. But, this time the wolf never moved.

Finally the little turtle came down the hill, got to where the wolf was lying and kicked him a little. The turtle said, "Hi, wake up." But the wolf never moved. So the little turtle began to sing, "Wolf, wolf, your bones will be quivering, the flies will be buzzing and buzzing around you."

All the little turtles came from their holes on the hillside where they were hiding when the wolf was hopping over them. Little turtle sang again to the wolf, "I told you I was little and can't run fast, but I can outsmart you."

Little turtle started singing again, as all the little turtles went off on their own, leaving the wolf alone, lying beneath the big tree, with the flies buzzing and buzzing around him.

THE MICE AND THE BAD ANGEL

"This is one of my favorite legends. We used to make our mother tell us this one over and over and over and over. I love the song in this one. We'd be under the mosquito net and would cover our heads when it got scary. But, when my mother would finish the story, we were supposed to sit up and spit four times. We didn't really spit, but made a spitting noise. If we didn't do that, then my mother would know we were asleep. Then she'd go to sleep, too."

Lots of people live in this village. At one time there lived a woman among them who had two beautiful girls with long black hair.

One night they all went to bed. When morning came, the mother called out for the girls to get up. But there was no answer. When she went to look, the girls were lying very still. She thought they were very tired, so she let them sleep. The girls usually helped her, but this time the mother thought, "I'll go ahead and cook for the hunters by myself."

In the morning, after cooking and sending the hunters on their way, she went back to wake the girls. Again they were not moving — as if they were dead. The mother ran out yelling for help and many people from the village came over. But there was nothing anyone could do.

Far away lived a wise old Indian medicine man. A runner was sent to find him and ask what could be done. The runner reached the medicine man's camp and told the sad story about how the two girls were in a deep, deep sleep and couldn't be awakened.

The old medicine man said that the Bad

Angel had come and taken the little girls' hearts and returned high into the skyland. "Someone must go to the skyland and get them back, but you must be quick or they will die in four days."

The runner returned to the village with the medicine man's warning. All of the medicine men in the village were called upon but none could do anything. "Even a flying bird," said one, "cannot reach this place."

On the second evening, little tiny voices could be heard in the distance. "I can go get it. I can go get it." Many in the village heard the voices, but no one paid any attention.

By the third day, the mother was really upset. The day was drawing near when she knew her daughters would never wake up. While she was crying, the tiny voice came out again: "I can go get it. I can go get it."

The mother called out, "Who is it? Why is such a tiny voice calling out such things?" The people in the village had warned the mother: "Don't listen to them." But again the voices came, this time closer to the mother, saying "I can go get it. I can go get it."

"Come out," said the mother. "Come out here."

A little tiny mouse ran out. It paused and then jumped upon her lap and said, "I can go get it."

"All right," said the mother. "I have to believe in someone, so it might as well be you. Time is running out."

The tiny mouse called to another mouse and they both said, "We can bring them back!" So the mother told them to go away and the two mice went and disappeared.

A medicine man asked the mother, "What can they do that all the other wise things of the earth and air cannot do?"

"We'll see," said the mother. "I was on the edge and knew not what to do until these two tiny mice told me that they could do what no one else could do. I will sit by my girls the rest of the afternoon and through the night. When the sun comes up and the mice have not returned, then I will know it is the end."

Quietly, the mother went to her daughters' bedside. There she sat crying, thinking maybe the people of the village were right. "But why would those two little tiny mice come to me and lie," thought the mother. "No, they can't be lying. But, if they don't return and the sun rises, my daughters will be gone."

Confused, she cried silently. Then, from a distance, she heard a tiny voice singing.

The song went: "I said, mighty angel can't ever do anything to me — I am — I am — far away land and sky. I sing away and I'm bringing raw hearts back." The song repeated its verse over and over, getting nearer and nearer.

The mother sat and listened to hear the words more clearly. She just knew the little mice must have the hearts. Yet, the sun was just about to peek over the horizon.

The two little mice appeared carrying the hearts! The little girls' hearts were much bigger than the mice, but they carried them up onto the bed and threw them into the girls' open chests. When the sun came up, the girls awoke.

They were surprised to see their mother standing there with the two mice beside her. "Go and rest," the mother said to the little mice. "After you are rested, then you can eat the corn hearts in the garden."

When the mother told the village people what had happened, they made a promise: From this day on, whenever the little mice come to eat the corn hearts in the corn fields, the Indians will never chase them off. For they saved the lives of the two beautiful daughters when no one else could.

ORANGE GRASSHOPPERS

"A long time ago, these grasshoppers would come out on a certain month. Every year, in the spring, millions of them would appear, everywhere. We used to play with them. I never see them anymore. Not a single one."

Many years ago, during the early part of summer, a young orange-colored grasshopper roamed the grounds everywhere.

These grasshoppers would get into anything green. The people got so mad that anytime these pesky grasshoppers came around, they would be stepped on and killed.

As the years passed, the grasshopper population lessened. Meanwhile, when people died, they would rise on the third day, and there would always be more people around to step on and kill the grasshoppers.

The orange grasshoppers had a meeting to discuss what was happening and how soon there wouldn't be many of them left. Then one grasshopper came up with a solution: "You all know that people rise on the third day after they die. So we must get on top of the grave, before the third day, and jump up and down on the grave so they won't come out. This will make fewer people."

So, to this day, when people die, they don't come up from the grave like they used to. The orange grasshoppers beat them long ago.

ℙOSSUMS

"To us, the possum was an ugly animal. We called it sho-ge-hot-ke, which is Miccosukee for white pig. The Seminoles would never eat one, even though there were a lot of possums around. In those days, we never saw the armadillo, but they are everywhere today in Big Cypress."

Once upon a time the possum had the most beautiful tail. He loved to show off among the other animals. He'd say, "My tail is more beautiful than yours!"

Then one day some of the animals got tired of him showing off so they told him, "If you think your tail is beautiful now, it could be so much, much better and more beautiful that it would stand out among all the other tails around you. Everyone would be so jealous of you."

Possum started yelling, "Tell me, tell me, tell me how!"

So they told him, "See all the moss hanging from the trees? Get it all and wrap it around your tail for a few days and let it sweat. Then take it off and it will be the most beautiful tail you've ever seen."

Possum couldn't wait, so he ran up the tree and gathered all the moss he could carry and wrapped it all around his tail. Then he lay around for a few days.

But when he took it off, the saddest look came over his face. Possum's pretty tail had been ruined and all the hair had fallen off.

This is the reason why the possum has an ugly, ugly tail.

THE RABBIT AND THE LION

"I never saw a real lion until many years after I first heard this story. My mother told us a lion was like a big dog with long hair and a big fuzzy tail. The lion would eat any living thing and that is why the rabbit got rid of him. The first lion I saw was at a zoo in North Miami. I immediately remembered this story because the lion was exactly as I imagined it, exactly as my mother told us."

In the early days when the world was new, many animals roamed the lands. Among those animals was the lion. Wherever the lion went, if he saw a rabbit, all he had to do was pick it up and swallow it.

One day, the old rabbit said to himself, "If I don't do something about the lion, he is going to eat all the rabbits and there won't be any more of us around."

The rabbit tried to think of what he could do to get rid of the lion. He thought and thought and then started jumping up and down. "I know what I can do," said the rabbit, who was full of lies. "If I could get to the other side of the ocean and tie it to this side, I could get rid of the lion."

So the rabbit got a rope and tied it to the other side of the ocean and pulled the land closer and closer. Then he went in search of the lion. He saw him lying under a big tree, full from his dinner. The old rabbit jumped up and asked the lion how he was.

"Hi!" said the rabbit. "I bet I can jump further than you. I might be little, but oh how I can jump."

The lion laughed but the rabbit would not let him rest. Finally the lion told the rabbit that as soon as he jumped further, he was going to eat him.

They went to the water and the rabbit pointed to the rope and told the lion that he had tied the two lands together. The rabbit told the lion that he would loosen the rope and make it further apart and they would jump until they had a winner. So away they went jumping along.

The rabbit loosened the rope until the two lands were far apart and he knew he could jump no further. He told the lion to jump and the lion barely made it to the other side. Then the rabbit ran to get the axe and chopped the rope.

Away went the land to the other side of the ocean, and the lion with it. The rabbit got rid of the lion this way, and that is why we don't have lions on this side of the ocean eating rabbits.

_T_HE RABBIT AND THE SNAKE

"They call the rabbit cho-fo-lock-sah, the lying rabbit. Rabbit is always telling lies and getting away with it. Even Bugs Bunny today is like that. They always get the best of him, but he still lies. Every storyteller I've ever heard — even a woman I met from the islands — talks about the rabbit who is always in trouble. It is the way children are taught not to tell lies."

Once at a gathering while everyone was sitting around talking, a voice yelled in the background: "I bet I can do something you can't do." The old men yelled back, "Go on by, we don't want to hear you." But the shouter wouldn't stop.

After this went on for a while, one of the men finally yelled out, "What can you do that we can't do?"

"This is all," said the shouter, a rabbit who hopped over to the men. "You can hunt and kill things, but there is one thing you can't do." An old man yelled out, "Go ahead and speak."

"Way over yonder lies a big, big rattlesnake about eight feet long. I can tie his neck and bring him to you in a bag. You can't do that," said the shouting rabbit, as everyone laughed.

They wondered how he could do this since such a snake was so big and dangerous. "Away with you, you can't do this. Go bring the snake over to us and then we'll believe you."

So, hop, hop, hop went Shouter the rabbit toward the nearby river. He walked along the bank toward the rattlesnake, which was stretched out in the sun, beautiful markings all over his body. "Oh, oh," said the rabbit, "I almost didn't see you and I could have stepped on you!"

"Well," said the snake, "now that you've seen me, be on your way."

"Oh, I almost forgot," said the rabbit. "See all those people over there? They said you were a very short snake and not even as long as this string in my hand."

"Ha, ha, ha," laughed the snake. "I am much longer than that piece of string."

"Well, OK, then," said the rabbit, "stretch out and let me measure you and I will go back to tell the people how long you really are." The snake stetched out so the rabbit could measure him.

But this old rabbit was full of lies! He jumped on the snake's neck, tied the rope around him and put him in the bag. When he took the snake over to the camp where the people were, they were very surprised. All they could do was stare at the rabbit.

All of a sudden, the snake rolled out of the bag. One of the men yelled at the rabbit and asked him how he caught the snake. "I told you I could," bragged the rabbit.

"Yes, with his lies," said the snake, who told the old men the story of how the rabbit got him in the bag.

That is why, to this day, snakes eat rabbits.

THE TWO WOMEN

"My great Uncle Jimmy Gopher told me this story. This is another one where the rabbit's lies get the best of him. You'd think the rabbit would learn from all his bad experiences, but he never does."

One summer there was a great gathering for the Green Corn Dance, which is held every year. People would enjoy the evening dances and dress in their colorful clothes. And this was the one day when everyone and everything had one language and understood each other. The birds, animals and everything that lived thought this was the most enjoyable event of the year.

The animals cleaned themselves in the pools, canals or rivers so their coats would shine. Now they were ready for the dance!

One night Rabbit, full of lies, led the people. They thought he was a wonderful leader. He had many songs to sing. On the third day when the fasting was going on and everything was about to end, the rabbit was sitting on a log watching the dancers. He saw a medicine man make his wife comb her beautiful hair and part it in the middle. Her dress was beautiful and she followed the leader in their dance.

The medicine man went back to his camp and brought back a big, shiny tomahawk and hit his wife right in the middle of the head where her hair was parted. She then became two beautiful women who dressed alike and were excellent dancers.

Rabbit couldn't believe his eyes. "Oh my, oh my," said the Rabbit as he called his wife over. "Go put on your best dress, comb your hair and part it in the middle and dance behind the leader." Not knowing what had happened, Rabbit's wife did what he asked her to do. She parted her hair in the middle and started dancing right behind the leader.

Rabbit got behind his wife and, with the tomahawk, hit her on top of the head where the part was. It knocked her down and killed her.

All of the men saw what happened and grabbed the rabbit. The men then took their tomahawks, placed Rabbit's tail on a log and cut it off. Of course, Rabbit had been very proud of his beautiful long tail. But they threw the tail into the fire to burn.

Now we know why rabbits only have cottontails!

TWINS

"They used to be superstitious about twins. You would have to give one away, or let one die. It was considered too dangerous to have both twins in one family. Even today, that belief lives on among some and they will give one twin away. Together twins are thunder and lightning. Dangerous. One without the other is no problem."

Long ago there lived a man with his wife out in the Glades. The man was always gone hunting to bring home food. The wife was always home doing things like pounding corn, washing and sewing clothing and many other chores.

One day when the man left to hunt, the wife was laid up. She was now with child and couldn't do as much as before. She heard noises nearby. When she looked up, there stood a hungry panther staring at her. Without hesitation, the panther attacked and killed the wife, eating every part of her with the exception of her womb that held her baby.

When the man returned he saw what had happened and was saddened about the loss of his wife. He took her remains to the woods to throw away. But this womb was round like a ball, so he placed it in a bag. He then laid the bag in the hole where his wife used to pound corn.

Weeks went by until the womb broke open. There were two little boys who crawled out to look around.

Thunder came along and picked up the twin boys; they became lightning. In the sky they lived and became men of thunder. They learned to strike out whenever they became angry. Sometimes when the twins get real mad you will see lightning all across the skies.

So, the twins are scary people. That is the reason why, when twins are born, one is killed and one is kept. Or both have to be doctored. Sometimes, they give one away, keeping them apart so they won't be mean.

Never try to provoke twins, because it is believed you will get very sick and die if they get mad at you. Many traditional people still believe the twin boys are in lightning and are the fighters in the sky. That is why, when it's raining, with thunder and lightning, you must stay put under a chickee until the storm is over.

WHO CAN LIVE LONGER WITHOUT FOOD OR WATER?

"The snake can outlive anything. I am a member of the Snake Clan, and we have very few people left. If a person wants to wrestle an alligator, they must ask permission from a member of the Snake Clan. There is no more Alligator Clan, so the nearest reptile, the snake, must be asked for approval. If a Snake Clan member approves, then the person can wrestle the gator. If they don't get permission, they might get bit."

Once upon a time when the world was new, there was only one language.

During this time there was a panther, owl, buzzard and snake. They made a bet as to who could live without water or food the longest.

Panther said, "That's nothing, I can outlive you all any day." So they all agreed and set a date to start off the bet.

Snake said, "No panther, you are wrong, I can go longer than all of you." Panther, owl and buzzard all climbed onto a branch of a tree. The snake could neither fly nor climb so it just lay below the tree.

It was decided that in the middle of the night they would each make their own music, as well as during the day, to let the others know where each of them was.

The first night, owl started off in the middle of the night yelling. In the middle of the day panther cried out, buzzard buzzed out his yell and the snake rattled below. This went on for about a week.

Then one night owl couldn't make much noise. The buzzard couldn't be heard at all. The next day, the snake and panther went looking around and found the buzzard and owl lying flat on their backs. This left only two.

For a few more nights the two made noises. Panther was still up a tree and snake was still on the ground. Then one night about the second week or so, the snake rattled and rattled all night, but never heard the panther. Early the next morning, the snake went out and found the panther lying there dead. So it is the snake that can live longer without food or water.

WITCH OWLS

"You might not believe this, but many people really believed that certain individuals could turn into animals and do a lot of things. I remember some of the medicine men, like Ingraham Billie and Josie Billie — you were kind of afraid of them. You would never say one word bad about them behind their back. There was a respect, not like today's young people and the way they talk about their elders. When an elder came to visit, the young people were made to wait on them. People were even afraid of my grandpa when he came to visit, that is, before he became a Christian. A lot of people used to believe these things, but I guess most of us have gotten away from it now."

In a village lived a group of witchlike families that stayed by themselves. They did odd things and had odd ways. And they liked to eat the hearts and lungs of fresh meat, no matter what it was from.

At night, some of these witches turned themselves into owls and hunted for heart and lung. Other older ones stayed by the fire with iron skillets ready so the owls could throw the food on the fire before they changed themselves back.

One night, everyone was hungry, so the younger ones of this family all decided to go hunting. Before they changed into owls, they had to take out their own intestines and hang them on the trees so it wouldn't be so heavy to fly around.

This night, they all hung their intestines on trees and left to go hunting. But there were hungry dogs out hunting too, and they came upon all these intestines hanging from the trees. There were big dogs among the little ones, so they jumped up and brought all the intestines down, which they all ate, and then they left.

After the hunting was finished on this night, the owls returned with the fresh hearts and lungs they had taken from large animals and people. They threw it all into the hot skillets waiting on the fire.

But when they went to put their intestines back, they weren't there! They went out hunting them, so they could again turn back into people, but they had no such luck. They tried to eat, but the food went right through them. In a couple of days they all died.

So this ended the group of witches who turned into owls to kill many people and large animals.

THE VILLAGE

The Seminole Indians lived in chickees in a village in the Everglades. The chickees were placed in a circle with a place for fire in the middle. In the village, there were four or five families, all of the same clan: in-laws, mostly married children, uncles, aunts and grandparents.

Everyone cooked over the same fire. One chickee was the eating place where all the food was placed when the women cooked the meal. If there were many in this village, all men and boys ate first. The women and girls ate last.

There was always sofkee to drink. Sofkee is a drink made from corn, boiled down into a hot soup. Food always included meat such as deer or land turtles, birds or other wild game, sweet or white potatoes or rice, pumpkins, beans and fish. At one time, there used to be plenty of game in the woods for food. Whenever visitors came, food was always offered to them.

The fire was a place where everyone enjoyed visiting. You would see many older people sitting around talking for hours at a time, late into the night, drinking coffee or sofkee. After mealtimes, only drinks. Young persons were not allowed to sit in or visit with the older people. They would be told, "You are too young to listen. This isn't for you."

It was also understood that when visitors came, the children would pick up their food and let the visitors have their places at the table. If the children wanted more food, they could come back and get more, but if they were finished, they had to leave.

If children came with the visitors, the village children could either talk with them or take them somewhere to play until the visiting was over. Sometimes, if it was late at night, the kids would lie down and sleep until the parents woke them up to go home. Sometimes, during these visits, they could learn how to make Indian medicine if there was an Indian teacher among them.

Little Seminole girls played with dolls made from the big root of the iris. The little roots at the end looked like doll's hair.

When there was sickness, news or need of a doctor but no horse to ride, one person was picked to run to the next village. The Seminoles always had a runner to go and carry messages out to the villages.

SEMINOLE DO'S AND DON'TS

Crying Dog

If you hear a dog cry in the wee hours of the night, it means you are going to hear bad news. You must throw something at the dog to make it quiet down.

Pets

The Medicine Man must put medicine on dogs or cats if you have them as pets. They will make you sick if you don't do this.

Fishing

If you are going fishing, don't go around repeating, "I'm going fishing," because it is believed that a rabbit will overhear you and he will run to warn the fish: "Don't bite because you will be pulled out."

Fishing Pole

If you are working on your fishing poles, don't let the dog touch them, because it's bad luck and you won't catch any fish. Don't let anyone walk over your pole, or cross it. That will bring bad luck and you won't be able to catch fish.

91

Noise and Dreams

If you hear a strange noise in the house or outside, or you think you have seen a ghost or spirit, you must get the Indian Medicine Man to doctor you right away. The same goes for bad dreams.

Medicine

It is believed that if a person is mad at you, the Medicine Man can fix a medicine for you to use that will make this person forget all things and stop talking bad about you. Also, if a man and wife are mad at each other, medicine can help settle the differences.

Graveyard

Never look toward a graveyard when passing by. Never eat or sleep at a graveyard. If you look into a graveyard, you might see a figure standing there. If you eat when passing by, you may choke. If you sleep, it is believed your spirit might be kept by a ghost and you will die. If you should see something like a ghost or spirit in a graveyard, you are to walk very fast and leave the place. You should never run, as it is believed that the ghosts will get your spirit and you will die. Get the Medicine Man to doctor you right away.

Rainbow

When the rain stops and there is a pretty rainbow in the sky, you should never point at it. It is believed that your finger will never bend again.

Cooking

When an animal is killed and brought back to the camp, you must feed it to the fire before cooking and eating the meat. A piece of meat is cut off and thrown into the fire to burn. It is believed that if the fire is fed, you will never get burned.

Bear meat should never be cooked or eaten with salt on it. If you do, it is believed that you might be harmed by a bear when you are in the woods.

When chickens are killed, they should be held over the fire to burn off the fine feathers. This is done after the large feathers have been pulled out.

Turkeys are not eaten by some Indians who believed they were spirit birds and would make one sick.

Bedwetting

If children wet the bed after they have reached the age when they shouldn't, you must get a tree frog and hit it in its "private parts" four times, then let it go. The children will no longer wet the bed.

Hurricane

A large bird with a forked tail would come before a hurricane, flying in the storm's path. If the hurricane was going to be very, very bad, the bird would fly low. If the storm was not very strong, the bird would fly high. My mother told me this was the way the Indians knew the condition of the "Big Wind," as they called it. The bird has a grayish color on its wings, with a white bottom, and a long and forked tail. We were told we would never see this bird unless a big wind was on the way.

Death

When a mother died, her children had to be doctored by the Medicine Man. He would pour medicine on their head four times as they sat facing East. The children would usually go to their aunts or grandparents to live and their father was free to marry again. The father would bring home fresh meat for them.

There is a special tree whose leaves were used to make the mix that was given to all; it is like a nerve medicine. The Medicine Man carried some of the leaves around with him. It is forbidden for kin people to look in a looking glass or comb their hair at this time.

All clothing belonging to the dead person was bundled up and carried away. Only a few things were left, items the kin wanted or liked, and everything else was removed so there wouldn't be anything around to remind them of the dead.

When the things were carried away and the dead was buried, on the fourth day the Medicine Man gave everyone herbs he had mixed up and all of the older people cleaned up and everything was put away.

Animals

You should never play with wild birds as they will make you sick. You cannot own a cat until the Medicine Man has doctored it. When you hear owls yelling at night, you are not to answer them — if you do, they will carry your spirit away and you will die. If there are alligators by the water and they are making a lot of noise, this means there will be a hard rain sometime during the day or night. You should not sell rattlesnakes — if you do, the floods will come. It is believed that if you make fun of snakes and alligators they will bite you when you are near the water or in the woods.

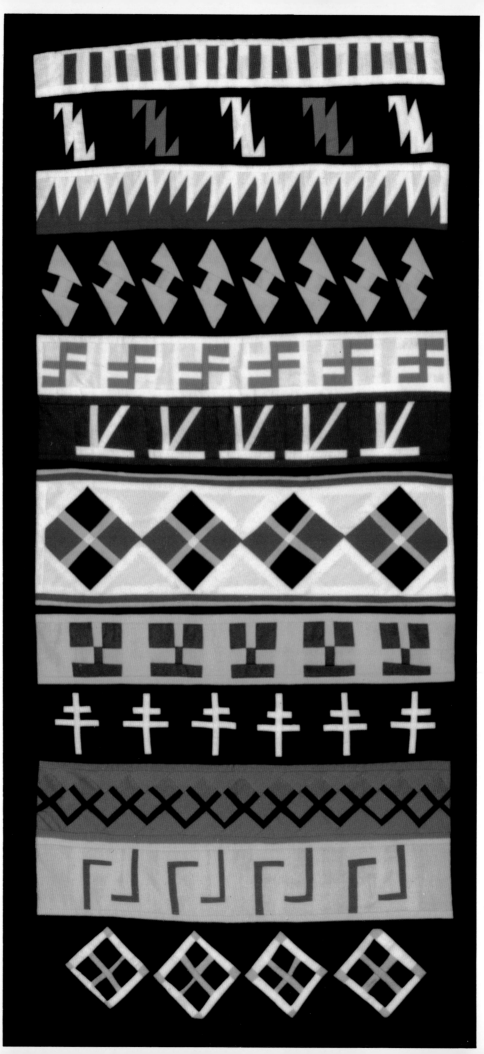

SEMINOLE PATCHWORK

Each strip of traditional Seminole patchwork portrays a special symbol. In this fabric, created by seamstress Connie Frank Gowen of the Hollywood reservation, the following symbols are portrayed:

Top to bottom

1   Rain
2)   Lightning/Thunder
3)   Fire
4)   Broken Arrow
5)   Man on Horse
6)   Bird
7)   Four Directions (Medicine Colors)
8)   Crawfish
9)   Tree
10)   Diamondback Rattlesnake
11)   Disagree
12)   Bones